TALESTER THE LIZARD

Story and pictures by John Himmelman

The Dial Press

New York

Published by
The Dial Press
1 Dag Hammarskjold Plaza
New York, New York 10017

Copyright © 1982 by John Himmelman
All rights reserved / Manufactured in the U.S.A.
First printing

Library of Congress Cataloging in Publication Data

Himmelman, John.
Talester the lizard.

Summary / Talester enjoys his home in a curled-up leaf over a small
pond because of the special friend who lives below him.
[1. Lizards—Fiction]   I. Title.
PZ7.H5686Tal   [E]   81-68775   AACR2
ISBN 0-8037-8787-1 / ISBN 0-8037-8788-X (lib. bdg.)

The art for each picture consists of a black line-drawing
with three overlays prepared in pencil and reproduced
in black, blue, and yellow halftone.

108688

To my Grandfather and Grandmother Himmelman

"There are great goings-on these days...."

Talester the lizard lived in a curled-up
leaf that hung over a small pond.

Like most lizards, he didn't like the water, but Talester lived there for a very special reason. Right below his home was the home of his friend, who also lived in a curled-up leaf.

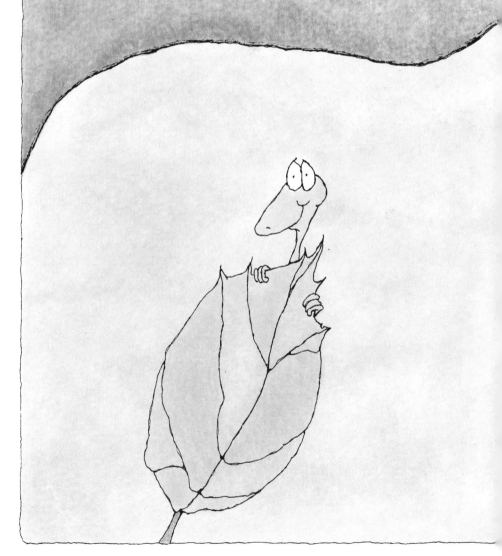

Talester would wake up every morning to see
if his friend was up, and he always was.

When Talester was happy,

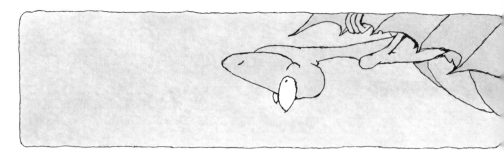

so was his friend.

When he was sad, his friend was too.

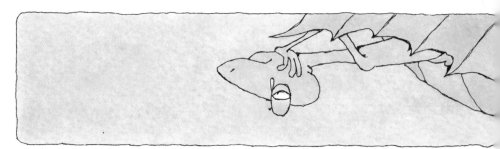

But Talester was hardly ever sad, because
he knew his friend would always be there.
It was nice to know that when he went out,
someone would watch his home.

Then something terrible began to happen. One hot, dry summer his friend started moving farther,

and farther,

and farther away.

Finally on one sad day his friend was gone.

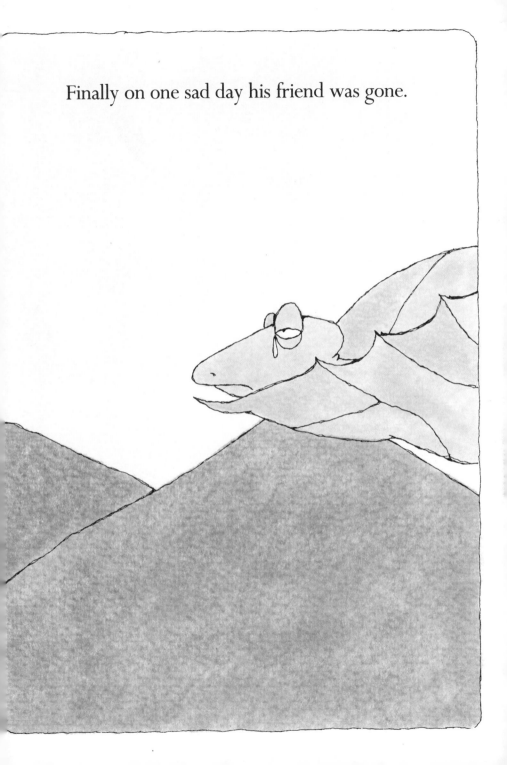

There was no one there to greet him when
he woke up,

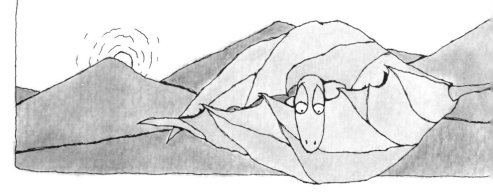

and no one to say good night to when
he went to sleep.

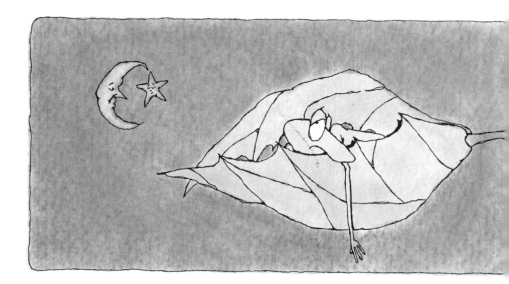

So one morning the lonely lizard decided
to leave his home and search for his friend.

He looked high

and low,

in

and out,
but his friend
was nowhere.

Talester's travels brought him to
the home of Joe the toad.

Joe listened patiently as Talester
described his friend.

"Why, he sounds just like you,"
exclaimed the toad.

"Oh, no," said Talester.
"We don't look a bit alike."
  He thanked him and went on his way.

Talester was growing tired, so he decided
to sit down on a rock for a short rest.
Suddenly the rock began to move.

He jumped off and discovered that he was
sitting on the home of a snail.
"I beg your pardon," said Talester, but
the snail smiled.
"That's all right," he said. "My name
is Simpson, Simpson Snale."

"My name is Talester," said the lizard
politely. After the two exchanged greetings,
Talester asked Simpson if he had seen anyone
that matched his friend's description.

The snail thought for a long time, and finally he said, "It sounds to me as if you described yourself!"

This time Talester blushed. "No," he said,
"he's a lot better-looking than me!"
He thanked the snail and went on his way.

Suddenly it began to rain.
Talester hadn't noticed the
storm clouds forming in the sky.
He didn't like to get wet,
so he ran all the way home.

By the time he made it, it was pouring.
Talester curled up inside his cozy leaf
while the rain fell throughout the night.

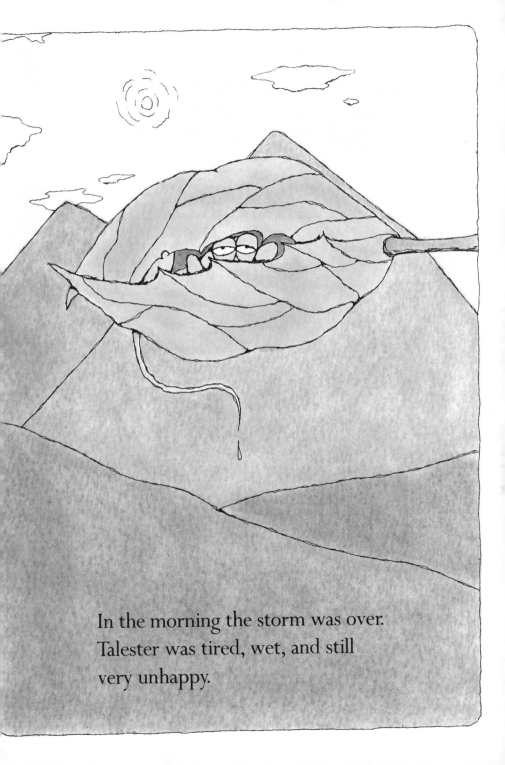

In the morning the storm was over.
Talester was tired, wet, and still
very unhappy.

He popped his head out of the leaf
and looked over the edge…

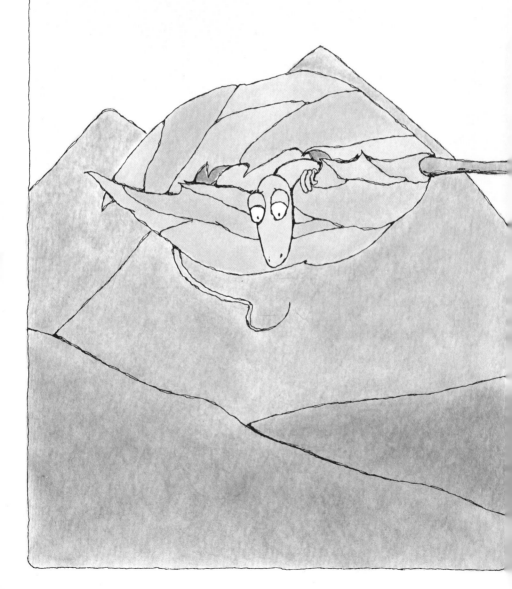

and right below him, with *his* head
hanging over *his* leaf, was his friend!
He was back!

Talester was very happy to see his
friend again…

and his friend was just as happy to see him.